2004

THIS WALKER BOOK BELONGS TO:

_____

_____

_____

_____

There are days when Bartholomew is naughty,
and other days when he is very very good.

First published 1998 by Walker Books Ltd, 87 Vauxhall Walk, London SE11 5HJ

This edition published 2000

© 1998 Virginia Miller

This book has been typeset in Garamond.

Printed in Hong Kong

British Library Cataloguing in Publication Data
A catalogue record for this book is available from the British Library.

ISBN 0-7445-7741-1

I LOVE YOU
JUST THE WAY YOU ARE

Virginia Miller

WALKER BOOKS

AND SUBSIDIARIES

LONDON • BOSTON • SYDNEY

One day Bartholomew was grumpy…
His ears were cold.

"Wrap your scarf around your ears
to keep them warm," said George.

But Bartholomew was still grumpy.
His legs felt too stumpy.

"I'll carry you," said George.

At home, Bartholomew's porridge was too lumpy,

his tummy too plumpy,

and he was too small.

"I'll feed you," said George.

At bathtime, Bartholomew hid.

He did not like anything at all.

"What a day," said George.
"You've been so grumpy,
your legs have felt stumpy,
your porridge too lumpy,
your tummy too plumpy
but Ba ..."

"I love you
just the way you are."

Bartholomew felt better. He kissed George,

and brushed his teeth all by himself.

"Time for bed, Ba," said George.
"We both need a little rest."

"Nah," said Bartholomew.

WALKER BOOKS

I Love You Just the Way You Are

VIRGINIA MILLER says of *I Love You Just the Way You Are*, "When the going gets tough for Bartholomew, it's comforting for him to know that George is always there for him – and will love him through all his moods. I hope parents will recognize the benefits and trials of love that Bartholomew and George share."

Virginia Miller, who also publishes under the name Virginia Austin, lived and worked in New Zealand before moving to England. The first children's book she illustrated, *Squeak-a-Lot*, was runner-up for the prestigious Mother Goose Award. It was followed by *Sailor Bear*, *Small Bear Lost* and *Kate's Giants*, as well as her own story *Say Please* and four other books about the bears Bartholomew and George, *On Your Potty!*, *Get Into Bed!*, *Eat Your Dinner!* and *Be Gentle!* Virginia lives in Bradford-on-Avon, Wiltshire.

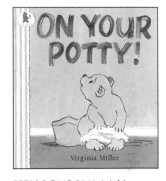 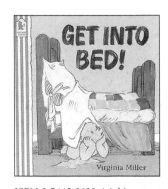 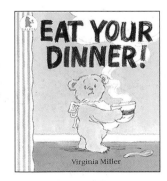 

ISBN 0-7445-3141-1 (pb)   ISBN 0-7445-3629-4 (pb)   ISBN 0-7445-3154-3 (pb)   ISBN 0-7445-6329-1 (pb)